NAVAJO
Coyote Tales

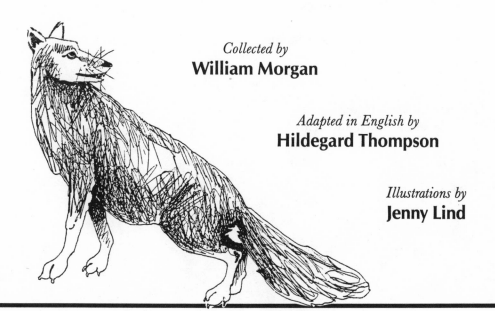

Collected by
William Morgan

Adapted in English by
Hildegard Thompson

Illustrations by
Jenny Lind

Ancient City Press
Santa Fe, New Mexico

International Standard Book Number:
ISBN 0-941270-52-1 Paperback

Library of Congress Catalogue Number:
88-072047

Designed by Mary Powell
Cover illustration by Jenny Lind

Translated by William Morgan and Robert W. Young

10   9   8   7

CONTENTS

INTRODUCTION

During the last decade or so many of the customs which formerly characterized the Navajo people have tended to disappear. Among these apparently dying customs is that of story-telling.

Not many years ago few Navajos had access to rapid modes of travel to visit neighboring towns. Few went to movies, or to other types of commercialized entertainment. In fact, few knew how to read and write for there were not many schools, and the white man's education was not always something to be desired from the point of view of the Navajo of former times.

But this did not mean that there was a complete lack of entertainment and instruction of the young. The old way of life maintained certain standards of right and wrong, and had certain non-material aspects about which each successive generation had to learn. And winter nights were long for a family gathered around the hogan fire. To shorten the hours of darkness, people wanted to remain awake as long as possible. So they achieved a dual purpose of instruction and entertainment by telling stories.

The story-telling period usually began in the fall, along about the time of the first frost, when the spiders, lizards, snakes, and other hibernating creatures had crept to their winter resting places. A child might be sleepy, but his father, grandfather, mother, or others of the older generation would awaken him and tell him to listen to a story. The story might take the form of history; it might tell of clan origins, clan interrelationships, or clan taboos. Again, it might be a portion of the legend connected with a certain ceremony. Often such stories as the latter served to instruct the young with regard to right and wrong, and many times the characters personified animals. The storyteller would use a high-pitched voice with a nasal quality to imitate the speech of the animals, much to the delight of the little folks in his audience. A story might illustrate the fact that the strong should not use their strength to take things from the weak. Whatever the moral, the narrator might enlarge upon it at the end of the tale to be sure that it was properly impressed upon the hearer.

This was Navajo education of a former day. "School was out" in the early spring when the days lengthened, and the various creatures came out of their winter hiding places.

The myths and legends of the Navajo have close analogy to the multitude of stories and fables which we inherited from our Greek, Roman, Celtic, and Germanic ancestors, and which have delighted and instructed countless generations of our people. Once upon a time our people could not read, so our stories were passed from generation to generation by word of mouth. Once, many of them were closely connected with the religions of our ancestors. These facts also apply to the Navajo.

The present book contains adaptations of several Navajo stories. Their purpose is to provide Navajo children, who are learning to read, with materials familiar to them. To keep the stories within the vocabulary level of children learning to read it was necessary to tell each story within a selected group of English words, and to repeat the selected vocabulary as much as possible. Consequently, the form and language of the tales vary radically from that which characterized the original version. But the subject matter—the theme of the narrative—is wholly Navajo.

ROBERT W. YOUNG
Specialist in Indian Languages

COYOTE AND RABBIT

One day Coyote was out walking.
He was walking in the forest.
He saw Rabbit.
He started to chase Rabbit.
Rabbit ran in a hole.
Coyote said,
"I'll get you out of that hole.
Let me think."
Coyote sat down to think.

"Now I know. I'll get you out.
I'll get weeds.
I'll put them in the hole.
I'll set fire to them.
Then you will come out," said Coyote.

Rabbit laughed.
"No, I will not come out,
    my cousin.
I like weeds. I'll eat
    the weeds."

"Do you eat milkweeds?"
    asked Coyote.
"I'll get milkweeds."

"Yes, I like milkweeds.
I'll eat the milkweeds," said Rabbit.

"Do you eat foxtail grass?"
    asked Coyote.
"I'll get foxtail grass."

"Yes, I like foxtail grass.
I'll eat the foxtail grass," said Rabbit.

"Do you eat rabbit brush?"
    asked Coyote.
I'll get rabbit brush."

"Rabbit brush? I like rabbit brush
    best of all.
I'll eat the rabbit brush, too,"
    said Rabbit.

"I know," said Coyote. "Piñon
    pitch."

Rabbit looked sad.

"You will kill me. I do not eat
    piñon pitch," said Rabbit.

Coyote was happy.
He ran from piñon tree
    to piñon tree.
He gathered piñon pitch.
He put the piñon pitch in the hole.
He set the piñon pitch on fire.
He bent low. He blew on the fire.

"Come closer," said Rabbit.
"Blow harder."

Coyote came closer.
He blew harder.

"I'm nearly dead," said Rabbit.
"Come closer!
Blow a little harder!"

Coyote came closer.
He blew harder.
He shut his eyes.
He blew harder.

Rabbit turned.
He kicked hard.
The fire flew in Coyote's face.
Rabbit ran away.
He was laughing very hard.

COYOTE AND THE FAWN'S STARS

Once Coyote was out walking.
He was walking in the forest.
He met a deer. She had her baby
    with her.

Coyote said, "Hello, my cousin.
What pretty stars your baby has
    on his back.
I wish my children had pretty stars."

Deer said, "Your babies
    can have stars.
I will tell you.
This is what I do.

When my babies are very little,
	I build a big fire.
The sparks from the fire make
	the stars.
You can do that for your babies.
Then they will have pretty stars, too."

Coyote was happy.
Now he knew what to do.
He wanted his babies
	to have pretty stars.
He gathered wood.
He made a big fire.
He put all of his children in the fire.
The sparks flew.
"Now they will have pretty stars,"
	said Coyote.

He danced around the fire.
Soon he said to Deer,
"Have they been in the fire
   long enough?
Will they have pretty stars now?"

"Yes," said Deer.
She ran away laughing.

Coyote took his children from the fire.
They were burned.
Coyote was angry.
He chased Deer.
Coyote still chases Deer, but he
   never catches her.

COYOTE AND CROW

One day Coyote was out walking.
He saw Crow.
Crow was holding his hat
  under his foot.

"What is under your hat?"
  asked Coyote.

"I have a bluebird under my hat,"
  said Crow.
"Will you hold it for me a little while,"
  asked Crow.

"I will hold it," said Coyote.

"Don't look under it," said Crow.

"Don't let the bluebird get away."

"I will hold it," said Coyote.

"I will hold it until you get back."

Crow flew away.
He flew behind a rock.
He could see Coyote, but Coyote
    could not see him.

Coyote looked all around.
He did not see Crow.
He looked at the hat.
"A bluebird," he thought.
"A nice bluebird.
Crow is gone.
I'll eat the bluebird."
He looked around again.

He raised the hat carefully.
He grabbed—but it wasn't
    a bluebird.
It was a cactus.

"Caw, caw, caw," said Crow from
    the top of the rock.

Coyote was angry.
He sat down to pick the thorns
    out of his foot.
"Caw, caw, caw," said Crow again
    and flew away.

 **COYOTE AND SNAKE**

One day Coyote was walking along.
He met Snake.
He said to Snake,
"Come to see me. Eat with me."

Snake said,
"All right. I will eat with you."
Snake went with Coyote.
He went into the hogan.
He wrapped himself around
 Coyote's fire.
He wrapped and wrapped and
 wrapped himself until he was
 in the hogan.

There was no room for Coyote.

Snake waited for Coyote to bring
    him some food.
Coyote was angry.
He was angry because there was no
    room for him in the hogan.

He got some old rabbit bones.
He threw them into the hogan
   to Snake.
He said,
"I forgot to tell you.
I was hungry, so I ate the meat.
I have only these bones."

Snake was angry, too, but he
   said nothing.
Soon he began to unwrap himself.
He unwrapped and unwrapped and
   unwrapped.
He began to go away.
He said to Coyote.
"Come to my house tomorrow.
Come to my house, and eat with me."

The next day Coyote got some
   cedar bark.
He made a long tail from it.
He tied it to his own tail.
Then he laughed to himself.
He thought,
"I'll get even with Snake."
He walked into the hogan.
He wrapped his tail around him.
He wrapped and wrapped and
   wrapped until his tail was
   in the hogan.
There was no room for Snake.

Snake got an old dead mouse,
   and threw it into the hogan
   for Coyote.

Coyote was very angry.
He said,
"An old dead mouse.
I will not eat
    an old dead mouse.
I would eat a snake before I would
    eat an old dead mouse."

Coyote began to unwrap himself.
He unwrapped and unwrapped and
    unwrapped.
He started home.
Snake put the end of Coyote's trail
    in the fire.
It began to burn, but Coyote did
    not know it.

Coyote walked on.
His tail burned very slowly.

When Coyote was almost home he
    smelled fire.
He thought it was the fire in his hogan.
He said to himself,
"Good. My fire is still burning.
My hogan will be warm."
He started in the door.
Just then the fire burned Coyote's
    own tail.
The bark was all burned up.
Coyote ran over the hill as fast as
    he could go.

Now Coyote never goes to
    visit Snake.

COYOTE AND
SKUNK WOMAN

One day Coyote was walking along.
He was walking in an arroyo.
The sun was very hot.
It made Coyote very hot.

Coyote said,
"Cloud come up!
Cloud come up!
Cloud come up!
Cloud come up!"
And a cloud came up.

Then Coyote said,
"Rain on me!
Rain on me!

Rain on me!
Rain on me!"
It rained on him a little.

Then Coyote said,
"Rain cover my feet!
Rain cover my feet!
Rain cover my feet!
Rain cover my feet!"
The rain covered his feet.

Then Coyote said,
"Rain cover my knees!
Rain cover my knees!
Rain cover my knees!
Rain cover my knees!"

The water covered his knees.

Then Coyote said,
"Rain cover my belly!
Rain cover my belly!
Rain cover my belly!
Rain cover my belly!"
The water covered his belly.

Then Coyote said,
"Water carry me away.
Carry me to many prairie dogs!"
The water carried him away.
The water carried him to many
    prairie dog holes.

Then Coyote said,
"Water leave me here!"
And the water left him.

Skunk Woman came to get water.
Coyote said,
"Sssst.
Sssst.
Sssst.
Sssst."
Skunk Woman saw him.
"Go tell everyone I am dead.
Tell them to come and see!"

Skunk Woman started out.
She met Rabbit.

She said, "Hello, Younger Brother.
Have you heard the good news?
That no-good Coyote is dead!"

Rabbit said, "I can't believe it!"

Skunk Woman said,
"He is dead.
His body is down by the river.
I saw him.
Go see for yourself!"

Rabbit started out.
He met Porcupine.
He said, "Coyote is dead.
Skunk Woman told me.
His body is down by the river.
Come on, let's go look at him!"

They started off together.
They met many prairie dogs.
They said, "Coyote is dead.
His body is down by the river.

Come on, let's go look at him!"
They all went along.

Coyote whispered something to
    Skunk Woman.
She went to meet the animals.
She said, "See, that No-good
    is dead.
Let us dance."
All the animals danced around
    Coyote.

Then Skunk Woman said,
"Let's look at the sky."
All of the animals looked
    at the sky.

Skunk Woman raised her tail.
She filled the air with her scent.
It got in the eyes of all the
    animals.
They could not see.

Coyote jumped up.
He helped Skunk Woman.
They killed all the animals.
They built a big fire.
They put the prairie dogs to roast.
They sat down to wait.

Coyote said, "Let's race
    to the mountain and back
    while our prairie dogs roast.

I can run fast, so you can
    start first."

She ran toward the mountain.
She hid in a hole.
Soon Coyote ran by very fast.
Skunk Woman came out of the hole.
She ran back to the fire.
She pulled the prairie dogs
    out of the fire.
She cut off the tails
    and stuck them in the ashes.
Then she ate the prairie dogs.
She crawled in a hole and went to sleep.

Coyote came back.
He said,

"I will eat the prairie dogs
    and hurry away
    before Skunk Woman comes back."

He pulled out a tail, and another tail,
    and another tail.
"Why that no-good Skunk. She didn't
    race at all.
She ate all of the prairie dogs."

Coyote was angry, but he tried
    to be sweet.
He said,
"Where are you, my cousin?
Where are you, my cousin?
Where are you, my cousin?
Where are you, my cousin?"

"Here I am," said Skunk Woman.
   "I am in this hole."

"Give me some of the prairie dogs.
   I am hungry," said Coyote.

"Your part is in the fire. Aren't they
   done?" said Skunk Woman.

"These are tails," said Coyote.

"Well, you can have these bones, too,"
   said Skunk Woman.

Coyote picked up the bones.
He ate the bones and the tails.
That was all he had to eat.

COYOTE AND
HORNED TOAD

Horned Toad was a good toad.
He worked hard.

He caught flies and bugs.
Everybody liked Horned Toad.

Even Lightning liked Horned Toad.
Horned Toad had
    a good farm.
He had a clean hogan.

He worked hard on his farm.
He raised corn and squash.

One day Coyote was walking around.

Coyote heard about Horned Toad.
He heard about
    his good farm.
He heard about his clean hogan.
He said,
"I'll just go over there and
    look around."

Horned Toad saw him coming.
Horned Toad was polite.
He did not let Coyote know
    he was watching.

Coyote walked right up to the hogan.
He said,

"My friend. My cousin.
We have been playmates.
I heard that you lived here.
What a clean hogan you have."

Horned Toad
    said nothing.
He just looked at Coyote
    and blinked his eyes.

Coyote walked around the hogan.
He started to pull things out.
He said to Horned Toad,
"This place is really mine.
This clean hogan is mine.
This good farm is mine, too."

Horned Toad's eyes got big.
Horned Toad said,
"What do you mean?
This hogan and farm are mine.
My children and I did all of this work.
We built this hogan.
We cleaned the fields.
We planted the corn and squashes.
You never do anything.
You just walk around."

"Get out," said Coyote.
"Get out or I will eat you."

"I won't get out,"
    said Horned Toad.
He swelled and swelled.

He swelled big enough to burst.
He said again,
"I won't get out."

"Then I'll eat you up,"
    growled Coyote.

Horned Toad swelled some more.
He swelled bigger and bigger.
He said,
"Go ahead. Eat me up."

Coyote showed his teeth.
He growled and showed his teeth
    some more.
He jumped at Horned Toad.
He gulped him down.

Then he went outside
     to walk around.
He said to himself,
"What a good farm I have!
What a clean hogan I have!"

After a while he went back
     into the hogan.
He lay down to sleep.

He heard something.
It said, "Ssst."

Coyote got up. He listened.
He heard it again. It said, "Ssst."

Coyote walked around.
He said to himself, "I wonder what
    that is?
Maybe this hogan is haunted.
Maybe somebody died in this
    hogan."

Coyote ran outside.
He looked at his side.
He said, "There is something rough
    in my stomach. It hurts me."
He walked about some more.
He felt worse.

He heard something again.
It said, "Ssst."

Coyote put his tail between his legs.
He ran into the hogan.
He ran around and around.
He howled and howled.
"Who's there?" he howled.

He heard it again.
This time it was louder.
It said, "Ssst."

Coyote ran in and out.
He ran like he was mad.
His tongue came out.
He kept saying,
"Who's there? Who is it?"

Finally Horned Toad answered.

He said,
"I am inside of you, you rascal.
I am scratching inside of you.
I am making that noise—
    ssst—ssst."

Coyote howled,
"Please come out, my friend.
Please come out, playmate.
I'll give you back your clean hogan.
I'll give you back your farm.
Please come out!"

"No, no," laughed Horned
    Toad.
"You ate me. You wanted me in here.

Now I'm going to look around
   some more.
Now I'm going to scratch again.
   Ssst! Ssst!"

Horned Toad looked at Coyote's
   liver. He pulled it.
He scratched it. "Ssst! Ssst!"

He walked up to Coyote's heart.
He pulled it. He scratched it.
"Ssst! Ssst! Ssst!"

He walked up to Coyote's lungs.
He pulled them hard.
He scratched them very hard.
"Ssst! Ssst!"

Coyote ran as fast as he could go.
He ran off Horned Toad's
   farm.

Horned Toad crawled up
   to Coyote's windpipe.
He choked Coyote.

Horned Toad said,
"I don't want any devils
   on my farm."

When Coyote was dead,
   Horned Toad crawled out.
He said to the dead Coyote,
"See what happens when you try
   to take things from weak people!"

Other Titles in this Series

☐ *Indians of the Four Corners*, Alice Marriott,
A history for Young Adults.

☐ *Little Herder In Autumn*, by Ann Nolan Clark,
In Navajo and English

☐ *Sun Journey: A Story of Zuni Pueblo*, by Ann Nolan Clark

☐ *Little Boy with Three Names: Stories of Taos Pueblo*,
by Ann Nolan Clark

☐ *Mystery of Coyote Canyon*, by Timothy Green,
A thriller for Young Adults

☐ *Navajo Coyote Tales*, collected by William Morgan

☐ *There Are Still Buffalo*, by Ann Nolan Clark

☐ *Wolf Tales: Native American Children's Stories*,
edited by Mary Powell

Ancient City Press
P.O. Box 5401
Santa Fe, New Mexico 87502
(505) 982-8195